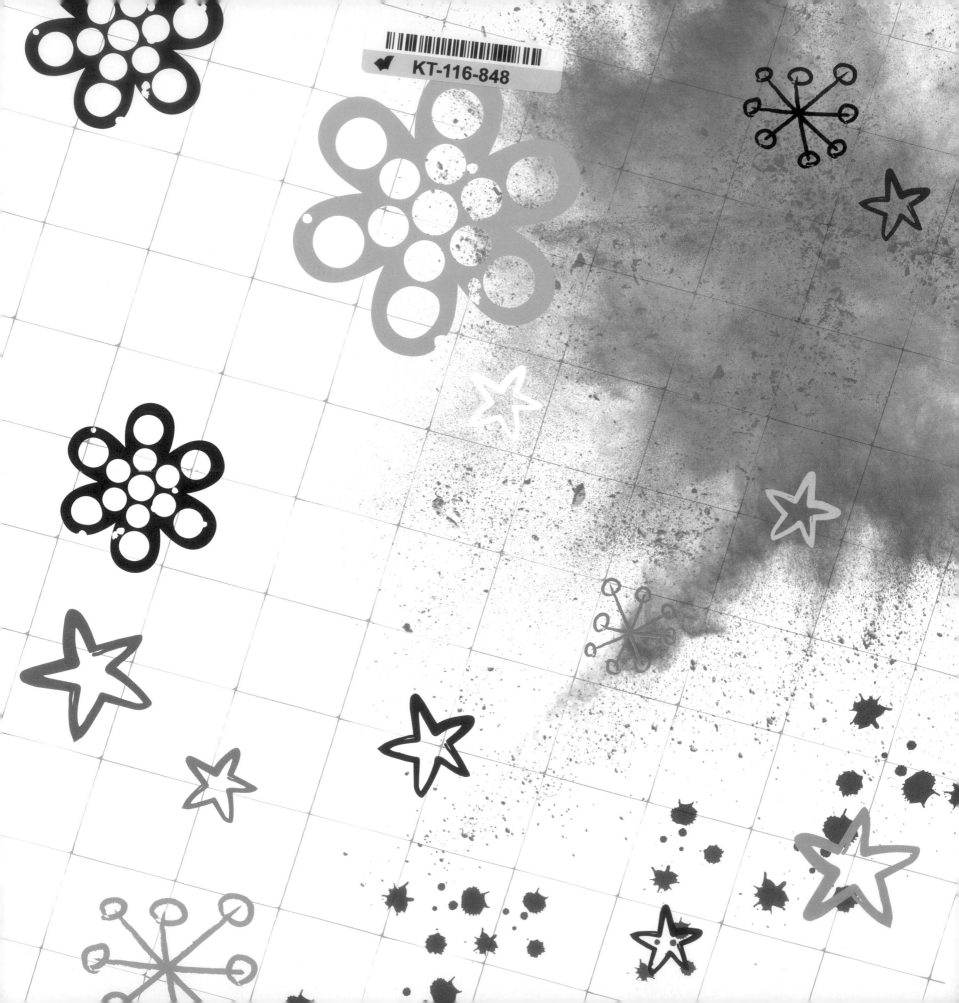

make believe ideas ltd

The Wilderness, Berkhamsted, Hertfordshire, HP4 2AZ, UK.
6th Floor, South Bank House, Barrow Street, Dublin 4, D04 TR29, Ireland.

www.makebelieveideas.co.uk

Written by Elanor Best.
Illustrated by Stuart Lynch.

CLUMP

THE LUMP OF COAL

WRITTEN BY ELANOR BEST

ILLUSTRATED BY STUART LYNCH

make
believe
ideas

CLUMP

Hey there, **Santa,** LISTEN UP!

I want to talk to **YOU.**

There's a PROBLEM with your **presents:** you DON'T **always** think things THROUGH.

Not EVERYBODY knows this:

I'm not just a **fossil fuel.**

When you get to **know me,**

I'm REALLY kind of **cool!**

You can USE ME as a **crayon**

to create the **darkest splat.**

I make a **smoky, SOOTY** trail— what **crayon** can do that?

Dear Santa,

for Christmas, I would like some new crayons.

COAL

I can ALSO be a **building block** that's STACKED UP to the **sky.**

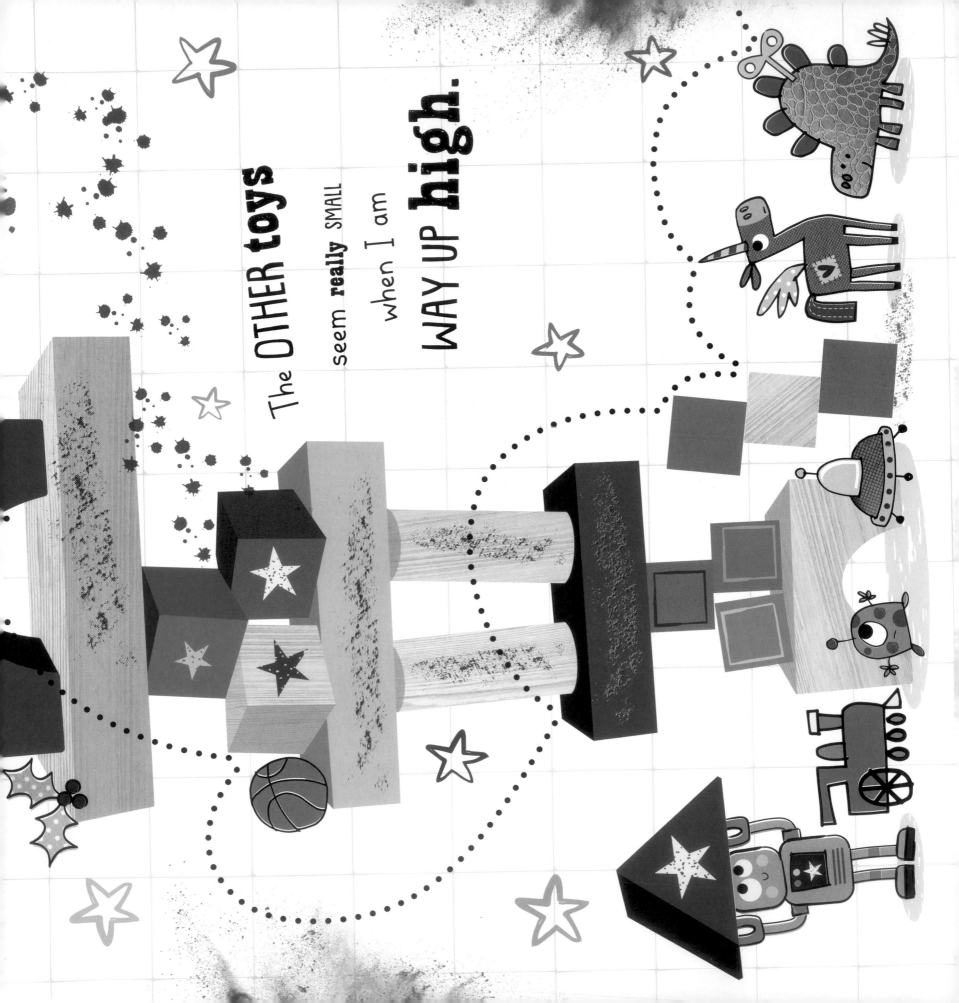

The OTHER toys seem **really** SMALL when I am WAY UP **high.**

I can EVEN be a
snowball
(that's just the WAY I ROLL).
But DON'T throw me at **children** . . .

...'cos I'm still a

lump of COAL.

In fact, I am so VERY **cool**, there is a case to MAKE for putting me in EVERY bit of **Christmas**.

(<u>NOT</u> THE **CAKE!**)

FLOUR

I can be a PAPER CHAIN . . .

. . . or HANG upon the **tree.**

And I'd make a **cracking** ANGEL,

come on,

SANTA,

can't you **see?**

I think I've RUINED **everything.** Just <u>LOOK</u> at all the **mess!**

I don't BELONG in **Christmas** even though I TRIED my **best**.

"Wait a moment,
little Clump!
It's me who got it wrong.
As Santa,
it's my job to get you
somewhere you belong.
Will you let me fix this,
and jump on board
my sleigh?
There's somewhere
I would like to go . . .

"...although it's far away."

"Let me introduce
you, Clump,
to friendly Mr Frost:
a snowman who has told me
about something that he lost . . ."

It's true!
It might sound silly,
but the shops are quite remote
and I feel incomplete without
three buttons on my coat.

And, Clump, you won't believe it but here's the funny twist:

every year,
a lump of coal
has been TOP of my list!

I've LEARNT that I am **different,** NOTHING like a **Christmas** toy.

My DIFFERENCE makes me **special,** and BRINGS others so much **joy.**

This book belongs to

....